第29屆奧林匹克運動會組委會
Organizing Committee for the 29th Olympic Games

國　色　氣　韻　盛　世　和　愛
National beauty charm Harmony and love of flourishing age

關玉良奧運藝術作品巡迴展組委會
About Organizing Committee for Guan Yuliang Olympic Art Works Exhibition Tour

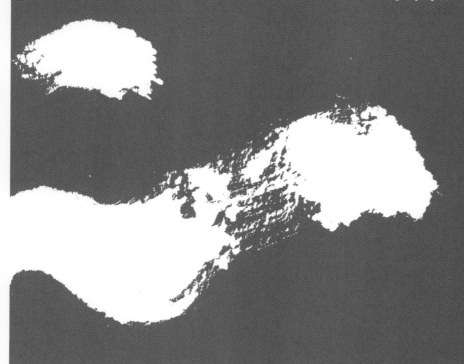

申辦奧運藝術巡展、這全過程
　　　　就是一件偉大的藝術！

The whole process of applying for a touring art exhibition in celebration of
the coming Olympic Games is itself a piece of artistic work!

　　　　　　　　　　　一大山2006於巴黎

　　　　　　　　　　　2006.10.16

謹以此書獻給我的祖國
獻給第29屆奧林匹克運動會
This book is dedicated to my motherland
and the 29th Olympic Games

如果失去崇高的道惪目標，就不能産生偉大的藝術。如果失去對生命本源的關照，也不可能産生舉世震撼的作品。如果藝術不能引導人們從冥冥中見到光明，不能向觀衆提出問題，不能表達可知世界的美學思想，那它只是沒有靈魂的驅殼。

Without lofty moral objective, there will be no great art to come into being. Without consideration on life source, there will be no heartshaking masterpieces created. In case that art fails to lead people from dark to bright, raising no questions to the audience, and unable to express aesthetic ideas of the known world, it is a mere work without soul.

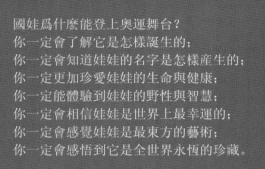

國娃爲什麼能登上奧運舞台？
你一定會了解它是怎樣誕生的；
你一定會知道娃娃的名字是怎樣産生的；
你一定更加珍愛娃娃的生命與健康；
你一定能體驗到娃娃的野性與智慧；
你一定會相信娃娃是世界上最幸運的；
你一定會感覺娃娃是最東方的藝術；
你一定會感悟到它是全世界永恆的珍藏。

Now the Chinese Baby (CB) mounts the Olympic stage;
You are sure to know how it came to birth;
You are sure to know how its name came about;
You are sure to cherish more the baby's life and health;
You are sure to feel the baby's untamedness and cleverness
You are sure to believe the baby is the most fortunate in the world;
You are sure to feel the baby is the art most oriental;
You are sure to realize that the pottery figurine baby is an article of
 everlasting worth in the world collection.

二十一世紀中國當代著名藝術家 · 關玉良藝術風

A FAMOUS ARTIST OF THE 21ST CENTURY CHINA THE ARTISTIS STYLE OF GUAN YULIANG

# DREAM OF 2008
# BIRTH OF
# CHINESE BABIES

圓夢

2008

國娃的誕生

黑龍江美術出版社

國娃的誕生 Naissance of Guowa
世界唯一器型 The Only Shape in the word
中國唯一的陶瓷娃娃 The Only china Baby in China

2

　　如果說北京奧運會、 中國當代藝術和公益事業是現今中國社會極具生命力的三條直線，著名藝術家關玉良先生就身處它們的交點之中。

　　《國色氣韻•盛世和愛—關玉良奧運藝術作品巡回展》大型系列公益展覽活動是充分展示中國藝術家喜迎奧運、祝福殘奧的高漲熱情和奧運情節；是通過藝術巡展的特殊載體，喚起全社會更多的人"參與文化奧運、關注殘奧運動、關愛殘疾人事業"；體現了藝術家關注奧運，關注殘奧的社會責任，是藝術家的藝術觀與人道主義思想價值觀的有機結合。

　　關玉良先生既是一位著名的藝術家，先後榮獲十多項國內外藝術成就大獎的殊榮；他也是一位熱愛公益事業的藝術家，多年來爲扶殘濟弱傾囊襄助。

　　關玉良爲巡展投入了極大的創作熱情和藝術情感。作品中有形態各異、造型豐富、活潑可愛，展示人的價值和創造力的陶藝中國娃娃；有體現出人生、人性審美情趣，從色彩、構圖、氣韻都有新的突破的水墨作品。關玉良先生爲迎接奧運和殘奧新作的300件藝術作品，承載著凝重的中華文化傳統和激越的奧林匹克精神，彰顯著先進的審美觀念和昂揚的時代激情。這些作品將人們帶向禮贊生命、向往和諧的意境，诠釋當代和愛精神和中華藝術創新精神。

　　兩個奧運，同樣精彩。2008奧運會及殘奧會不僅需要文明、和諧、歡樂的人文奧運氛圍，更需要通過殘奧會的舉辦，讓全社會了解"超越•融合•共享"的殘奧理念；讓更多的人讓走近殘疾人，真正地關愛殘疾人，關注殘疾人事業，推動殘疾人事業的發展。關玉良奧運藝術巡展活動就是在營造"關愛殘疾人、支持殘奧會"

的行動上做出了一個表率作用。體現了對人道主義的弘揚，彰顯著一種人文精神，爲中國的殘奧事業將留下一筆重要的文化遺産。

　　"關玉良奧運藝術作品巡展"是奧運文化重要項目之一，他用藝術積累诠釋了當今人類尋求"盛世和愛"的永恒精神的追求，他用藝術智慧讓中華藝術在奧運文化平台上又一次發揚光大。

　　我們相信，伴隨著文化奧運的傳播，關玉良先生的奧運藝術作品不僅是中國的，也會成爲世界的。

北京奧組委執行副主席
中國殘疾人聯合會理事長
二〇〇七年八月二十二日

世界唯一器型　中國唯一的陶瓷娃娃
The Only Shape in the word　The Only china Baby in China

# FOREWORD

Tang Xiaoquan

If we can say the following three things: Beijing Olympic Games, Chinese modern art and the magnanimous act for public good, represent three vigorous lines crossing each other in the Chinese society today, then we may say well that Guan Yuliang, the famous artist, is just found at the point of intersection of the three lines.

Beauty, Majestic Style, the Flourishing Age and love——This is the catchwords for Guan Yuliang's touring exhibition of artistic works in celebration of the Beijing Olympic Games. Such large scale activities demonstrate the Chinese artists' enthusiasm in greeting the grand meeting, in taking part in sports, in making contribution to the the Paralympic Games. This exhibition marks the integration of the artist's outlook of art with the humanitarian values. It will bring more and more people to show concern for the Paralympic Games, arouse great love for the disabled. Such a large scale movement will surely yield abundant results in creating a humanitarian atmosphere concerning Olympic Games, that of civilization, harmony, gaiety, friendship and love, and in elevating the self-confidence, self-strengthening and renewal of the Chinese art in the arena of the world. It shows the Chinese artists' expectation of the grand event. It is of great significance in publicizing the Olympic Games, and the Paralympic Games.

Mr. Guan Yuliang is an artist renowned both at home and abroad. He is now a professor in the art college under Shenzhen University, a first grade artist. He has won more than 10 major prizes for his achievements in art; He has held more than 30 art exhibitions at home and abroad, and has published more than 20 books, painting collections and personal monographs on art. His creation involves a wide range, including sculpture, pottery art, heavy color, inkwash, etc, besides; Mr. Guan is also an artist active in magnanimous act for public good.

One of the artistic works to be displayed at Guan's planned touring exhibition will be pottery figurines of Chinese Baby (CB). They are quite diversified in form, bearing, and rich in modeling, vivacious and lovely. They reveal the value of life and creativeness. There will also be inkwash showing the Chinese aesthetic taste, with an artistic breakthrough in coloring, structure, style, etc. The roughly 300 artistic articles of best quality are all created specifically in celebration of the 2008 Olympic Games, and that of the disabled. In creation of these articles, either pottery art or inkwash, Mr. Guan Yuliang, while retaining the basic national aesthetic taste, employs a diversity of techniques and forms, maximize the integration of the unique charmingness in the coloring of Chinese inwash with its unique modeling. In this way, Guan tries to bring a brand new artistic style into China's inkwash art and into the modern pottery works, thus bringing forth artistic works of the Chinese style and Chinese grandeur. These artistic works carry stately the Chinese cultural tradition, give prominence to the advanced, aesthetical conception and the high-spirited passion of the time. These works pay high tribute to life and harmony; give interpretation to the new spirit of friendship and love. They make such human aspiration sublime as "transcending oneself, striving for perfection, sharing and melting into one". They represent a successful combination of inkwash, sculpture and pottery with the modern western artistic ideas.

The planned touring exhibition will not only blaze a trail in this respect, something rare in its scale, but also in the large areas it covered. It may well be compared to a new long march for China's modern art.

This new long march of art will not only open up a new path for spreading the Olympic art, but also, more important as it is, open up a novel path for passing on people's loving heart, trying our best to call on more people to take part in the cultural Olympic, artistic Olympic, carrying forward the Chinese spirit of kindheartedness and harmony.

"Guan Yuliang's art in the name of Olympic" carries not only the century long passion and tears of the Chinese sons and daughters, but also the great expectation for our national rejuvenscence. What it brings to people is not only the exhibition unprecedented in Olympic history, but also to enhance and glorify once again the Chinese art in the history of world civilization. At the same time, it also implies an interpretation of the meaning and value of life, of the perpetual pursuit of "a flourishing age and love". It embodies the Olympic ideal: "Transcendence, Melting into one and Sharing".

The present touring exhibition in the name of Olympic is a valuable attempt of the Chinese artists, with their sincere love and their self-confidence in the Chinese culture, in looking for resonance in art and culture in face of the whole world.

Mr. Guan Yuliang is fortunate. His works belong to the modern art of China, and also to that of the world. Our good wish to him!

(Tanslated by Profeessor Pan Zongqian)

國娃的誕生 Naissance of Guowa 世界唯／造型 中國唯／的陶瓷娃娃 The Only Shape in the word The Only china Baby in China

# 國 娃 的 誕 生

馮國文

　　國娃，是一組憨態可掬的陶藝雕塑作品，它渾然天成，動靜有度，靈活而不張揚，是藝術家關玉良對人類生命力量的一種想象和解讀。

　　作爲獻給2008年北京奧運會的一組陶藝雕塑藝術作品，藝術家沒有選擇速度與力的對抗一類的現代體育視覺符號，做直接的表述，而是借助豐腴的體態，來傳遞生命的可愛，讓稚拙的肢體，來傳達生命的情趣；面部，則是大象無形，略去了所有的細部，然而，對自身的依戀和陶醉的神態，讓人領悟到對自我的健康與快樂的欣賞，是一種別有洞天的生命境界，這才是人生原本該希求的。這是藝術家對人文奧運本質的深層次理解和獨特體現。這也是藝術家本人一貫的理念。

　　20多年前，結識玉良，第一次看到他的繪畫作品，在滿幅郁郁蒼蒼的墨氣之中，若隱若現的藍眼睛、綠眼睛，甯靜的注視著畫外。20年了，這甯靜的注視，依然沒變，其實，那就是藝術家本人的目光。那目光，其實就是藝術家甯靜如水的心靈世界。

　　20年後的今天，國娃的誕生，仍然延續了這種大音稀聲的靜默。盡管這期間，藝術家進行了紙媒體上的墨像——墨彩——文字系列——人體系列等創作，在雕塑方面有了陶——俑等一系列探索，但是藝術家的生命體驗，似乎愈發的甯靜和寬容，這之間產生的廣博，就帶有一種俯視世界的大氣。

　　我在想——國娃，作爲一組陶藝雕塑作品的誕生，其實，是藝術家對人的生命演化過程的一次感悟。

　　國娃——它，原本是一捧泥土，是天地靈氣，與藝術家心靈契合而後成型，借火的煅燒，完成了一個生命的胚胎，在藝術家的東方情懷裏；它，染上了民間色彩，印上了國花牡丹的肌膚，這是藝術家民族審美取向通過釉彩的一種外化，這是一種積極向上的中國式的生命大寫意，它體現了一位現代藝術家的品位。

　　再過20年，我們走在路上的雙腳，因生命的老化，也許不再鏗鏘，但是，我們回望世界的目光，會更加明亮，因爲歲月的智慧已經貫注進了我們的心底，明察秋毫，靠的不是眼睛，那時，我們還能看見國娃。

　　那之後的許多年，也許我們已經不在這個世界，因爲那是自然的法則。但是，玉良的國娃還在。它，在中華民族21世紀的那次盛事中誕生，因爲它是藝術，所以它會永恆。

　　玉良、你、我，今生苦苦追求藝術，因由很多，也許是家傳，也許是藝術之光照耀過我們的心靈，印記太深，但是，結果只有一個——如果你和我也都有玉良這樣的國娃傳世，那個隔世的黃昏，那些來世的人們，用目光打量和欣賞國娃的時候，我們就會欣慰。

# The birth of Guowa

Guowa is a group of darling sculptures defined by a natural, flexible but not publicity. They are artist-Yuliang Guan's imagination and interpretation to the force of human life.

As a sculpture works dedicated to the 2008 Beijing Olympic Games, the artist has not expressed directly by using the confrontation between speed and force - modern sports visual symbols. Rather than transferring the lively and interesting life though the plentiful body and simple limbs. The face is not clear for omitting all the details. However, the attachment on its own and intoxicating manner make us realize that the admiration to self-health and happiness are distinctive life realm, which is we should desire.

They are the artist's deep-rooted understanding and unique expression to the nature of the Humanistic Olympics

They are also the artist's constant ideas.

More than 20 years ago, we became acquainted with Yuliang when we first saw his paintings. In the paintings filled with luxuriant edge, the partly visible blue eyes and green eyes gazed at the outside of paintings quietly.

20 years have passed, the tranquil gaze remain unchanged. Actually, that is the artist's vision. That vision, in fact, is the artist's tranquil spirit world.

20 years later, the birth of Guowa has still continued the static touch.

Although this period, the artist has embarked on the creation about the ink and wash paintings on paper, color ink, paintings, characters and human body series, and in the aspect of sculpture made some exploration on the ceramic and puppet, the artist's life experiences seemed more tranquility and tolerance. The vast generated form here had an atmosphere of looking down upon the world.

I was thinking -- as a sculpture works, Guowa actually is the artist's understanding to the evolution of human life.

Guowa is a handful of soil originally. By combining the heaven - earth spirituality and the artist's soul, it took shape and formed a life embryo though fire. In the artist's oriental mood, it caught the folk color and the flesh of peony, which is Chinese national flower. This is an expression of his national aesthetic orientation though glazing and a positive life enjoyable with Chinese-style. It has manifested to us a modern artist's tastes.

In 20 years, the feet we walk on the road maybe no longer sonorous for the aging of life, but the vision we look back to the world will be brighter, because the wisdom of years has immerged into our hearts. Discerning people does not rely on eyes. Then we will see Guowa again.

Many years later, perhaps we have not been in this world, because it is a natural law.

However, Yuliang's Guowa still exists. Because it is born in the events of Chinese nation in the 21st century and it is art, so it will be eternal.

Yuliang, you and me, may have many reasons to pursue art sincerely in our whole lives.

Perhaps family or the art light shining off our soul result in deep imprint.

But there is only one result-if you and me all have the art works like Yuliang's Guowa to be handed down for generation, we will be pleased when the people appreciate Guowa in the future evening.

面對藝術的海洋，你去吧，不要問爲什麼，也
不要說它是什麼，一切美好的幸福感，都在你心裏
得到體會，爲了這份體會你會永遠地創造著……。
你會永遠地感受幸福，因爲你永遠在創造幸福的過
程中。

關玉良
2003.3.23

Facing the vast field of art, you may as well
go your own way, without asking why, or what.
you are well conscious of the happiness in your
heart. Inspired by this divine happiness, you will
keep on working creatively without end. You
will be constantly experiencing the happiness
because you are found permanently in the
process of creating happiness.

Guan Yuliang
Mar 23. 2003

我参与我就我快乐

玉良〇八岁书

The Only Shape in the word 世界唯一／器型　The Only china Baby in China 中國唯一／的陶瓷娃娃

【國娃】陶瓷之一
95CMX30CM
2006 年

9

【玉娃】 國畫
55CMX45CM
2005 年

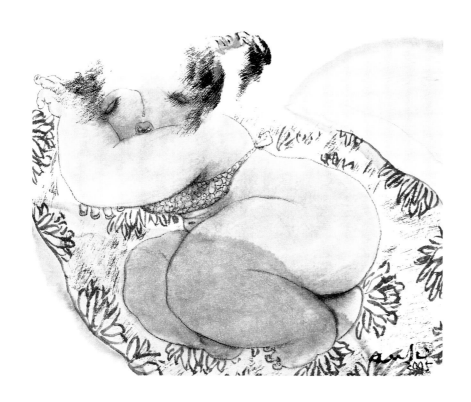

【山娃】國畫
55CMX45CM
2005 年

　　如果說中國文化是一種獨特的文化存在於世界文化的版圖上，那麼中國藝術同樣是以區別於西方藝術的物質存在於世界藝術版圖上。

　　當代的中國藝術，不僅僅重視中國符號、中國技法，更爲重要的是需要呼喚中國藝術精神的回歸，並且在以中國傳統文化爲根基的基礎上，發展出中國自己的現代主義藝術。

【國娃】陶瓷之六
66CMX42CM
2006 年

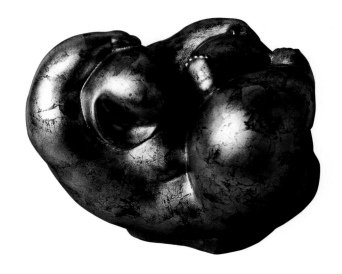

【國娃】陶瓷之七
30CMX27CM
2006 年

【國娃】陶瓷之八
50CMX48CM
2006 年

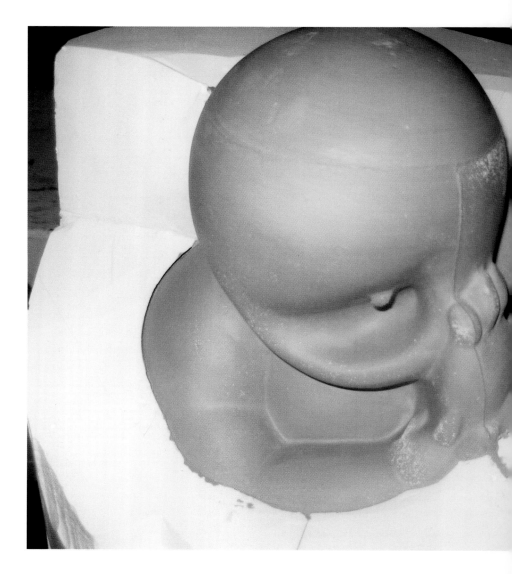

世界唯一／造型　中國唯一／的陶瓷娃娃

The Only Shape in the world　The Only china Baby in China

【國娃】陶瓷之九
60CMX48CM
2006 年

　　它是山裏的孩子——野孩子，不是都市裏的孩子，這樣的孩子活蹦亂跳，充滿生命力，活潑調皮，你看他們都是光著屁股，咧開嘴巴大笑，代表了我對未來中國人的一種期望。其次，他們身上都是地道的中國符號——牡丹花、中國紅，北京奧運傳達的首先應該是地道的中國文化。

【國娃】陶瓷之十一
83CMX40CM
2006 年

【月亮娃】國畫
55CMX45CM
2005 年

【國娃】陶瓷之十二
55CMX20CM
2006 年

【雅娃】國畫
55CMX45CM
2005 年

【國娃】陶瓷之十三
55CMX23CM
2006 年

【歌娃】國畫
55CMX45CM
2005 年

【國娃】陶瓷之十四
40CMX28CM
2006 年

　　寬大的畫室裏，有一群色彩豔麗、憨態可掬的雕塑娃娃，或坐或站，姿態各異，臉孔卻是抽象的，沒有鼻子、耳朵、眼睛，只有嘴巴傳神地表達著情緒，有的在怒吼，有的在大笑，有的狡黠，有的質樸。共同的特點是光頭、胖乎乎和身上充滿民族風情的豔麗花朵圖案。這些娃娃健壯、陽光，透出一種原始、野性、雄健、蓬勃的生命力。這組三十多種姿態、五十六種色彩的娃娃是關玉良獻給2008年北京奧運會以及殘奧會的一組陶藝雕塑作品。

【秋娃】國畫
55CMX45CM
2005 年

　　"這組娃娃是最當代，也是最傳統的。奧運精神最初的含義不是競技，而是強身健體，是倡導一種生命力量的展示和張揚。同時奧運文化又是一種大眾文化，必須通俗易懂。而娃娃是最具有活力的生命形態，我選擇了牡丹等色澤鮮豔的圖案，因爲這是一種最傳統的符號，我想用最傳統、最本原、最民族的方式來詮釋最當代的內涵。"

【國娃】陶瓷之十五
53CMX18CM
2006 年

【國娃】陶瓷之十六
28CMX30CM
2006 年

世界唯／一造型 中國唯／一的陶瓷娃娃
*The Only Shape in the word* *The Only china Baby in China*

　　要建立中國人對於自己民族文化的信心，需要幾代人的共同努力才能完成，我現在能做的就是努力做好自己的事情，讓民族文化通過我們這代人傳承下去。奧運藝術展就是這樣一次傳承，如果其中能有我的一些創造性的貢獻，那是我的夢，是圓了我2008的夢。

【嬌娃】國畫
55CMX45CM
2005 年

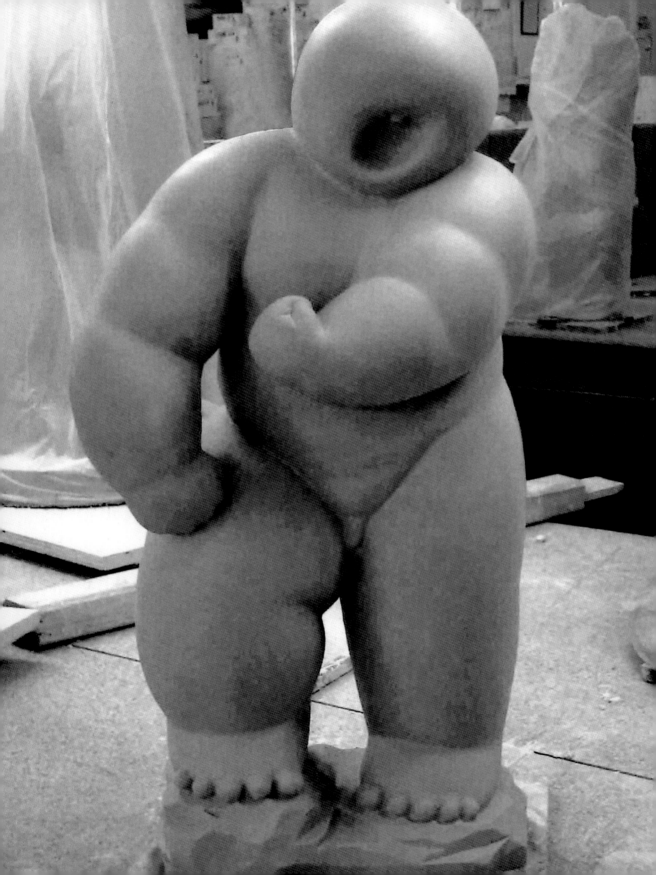

全方位的藝術跨越，反映他對社會發展的思索。

天才的藝術家是以大象無形來觀察、把握、感悟，重新組合這個世界。

【牛娃】國畫
55CMX45CM
2005 年

【英娃】國畫
55CMX45CM
2005 年

【國娃】陶瓷之十七
48CMX23CM
2006 年

【國娃】陶瓷之十八
95CMX30CM
2006 年

【睡娃】國畫
55CMX45CM
2005 年

【鐵娃】國畫
55CMX45CM
2005 年

【國娃】陶瓷之十九
66CMX42CM
2006 年

　　從某種意義上說，藝術應該是藝術家對社會所盡的一種責任，也應該是他們對人類的生存與社會發展的一種關注和看法。現代藝術應該充分反映人類現代的生存環境，這是現代藝術作品創作的源泉。畢加索之所以能成爲一代大師，就因爲他的作品代表了一個時代。

【泥娃】國畫
55CMX45CM
2005 年

【國娃】陶瓷之二十二
50CMX18CM
2006 年

【俏娃】國畫
55CMX45CM
2005 年

【國娃】陶瓷之二十四　　【國娃】陶瓷之二十三
30CMX28CM　　　　　　48CMX18CM
2006年　　　　　　　　　2006年

【奧娃】國畫
55CMX45CM
2005年

【國娃】陶瓷之二十四
90CMX30CM
2006年

【盼娃】國畫
55CMX45CM
2005年

【國娃】陶瓷之二十五
55CMX45CM
2006年

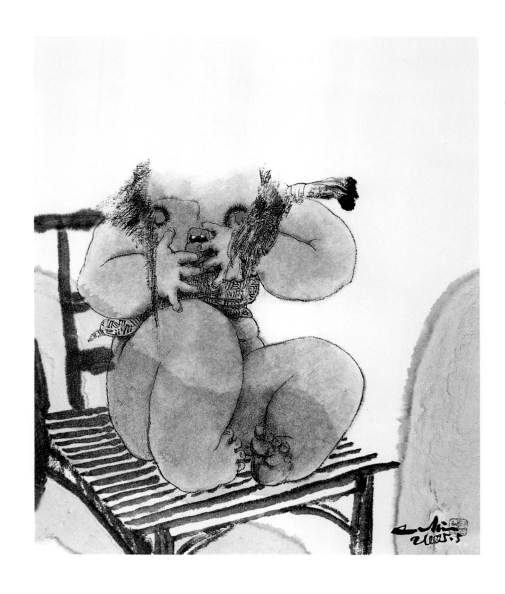

【慧娃】國畫
55CMX45CM
2005年

【國娃】陶瓷之二十六
55CMX22CM
2006年

　　對於藝術與人性兩者之間的關系，關玉良也有自己深刻的認識。他認爲藝術技法並非是藝術本質，技法通過一定階段的努力後，一般畫人亦可達到。而重要的區別就在於藝術家人性和品位的區別，藝術思想深度與審美觀的深度區別。對所有藝術家而言，不管他屬於何種派別，但都必須有一種自身健康、發展的規律。他們必須在民族文化的大框架下，隨著自身閱曆的豐富、人性與品味的發展而發展，其作品也應該是隨著藝術家精神的追求和人性的發展而日趨成熟的。

國娃的誕生 Naissance of Guowa

世界唯一／雕型　中國唯一／的陶瓷娃娃

The Only Shape in the word　The Only china Baby in China

【藝娃】國畫
55CMX45CM
2005年

中國娃

陶瓷女繪

【國娃】陶瓷之二十七
55CMX23CM
2006年

The Only Shape in the word　世界唯一造型　The Only china Baby in China　中國唯一的陶瓷娃娃

【陶娃】國畫
55CMX45CM
2005年

【國娃】陶瓷之二十九
55CMX18CM
2006年

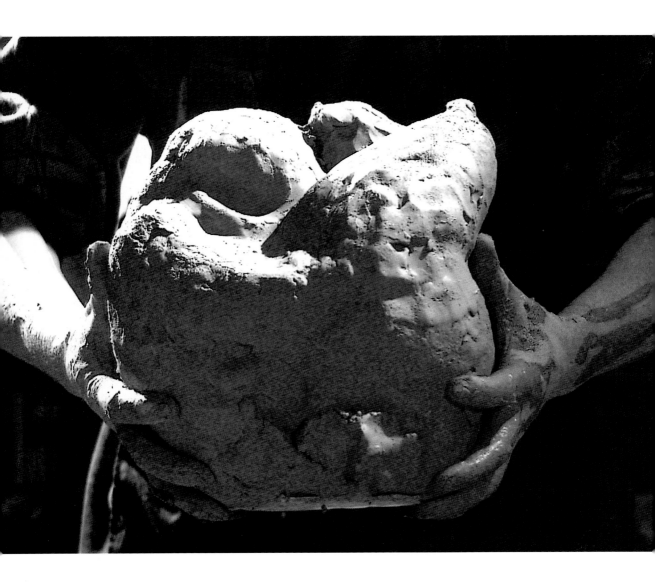

【夢娃】國畫
55CMX45CM
2005年

# 妙趣橫生的 "中國娃"

冬炎

被贊譽爲 "東方畢加索" 的中國著名畫家關玉良先生，他的任何一件作品都孕育著無限的豐富內涵和強不可擋的藝術生命力，給觀者以極爲震撼的視覺沖擊力。

2005年，關玉良創作的題爲 "中國娃" 的系列作品，更加豐富了畫家超人的想象力和超人的藝術表現力，使人歎爲觀止的是他妙不可言的藝術表現力。此系列畫作雖然題材同一，數量僅爲16開，但絕非有雷同和乏味之感，給懂得藝術欣賞的人士以發出妙極逸品之感歎——每幅作品耐人尋味的同時賦予人以超凡的無限返想——那臂彎裏持著竹籃，裝的是山野人家隨時可以采摘到的野果，憨態可掬的山裏娃那一上一下的翹角辮子，正是紡織的慈母一早用最爲豔麗的 "辮繩" 所精心紮就的，幼女口若含飴，咂摸品位著生活的新鮮與甜美；炎熱的夏季，竹席是最理想的臥具，一角肚兜罩在胸腹，安然入夢，角邊爲伴的是一只同樣閑適入夢的貓仔，幼女豐腴的肢體松弛懶散，儼然是一個不知世間愁與苦的稚童，她無憂無慮的田園般原始生活正是無數人們所企盼的 "夢幻仙境"；更有那在大自然中隨心所欲的翩翩起舞，與天空自由飛翔而過的小鳥天籟般的情愫共鳴，是人間最欲歡歌的暢想曲；女娃睜大著水汪汪的眼眸，透出寶石般純淨可愛的光芒，身旁的和平鴿與其一樣純淨曼妙，渴求人間的和平與和諧，女娃半張的小口似正待發出和平的呼喚……

關玉良的這套以兒童爲主題的畫作，如他的其他題材一樣，色彩斑斕、造型特殊，引領觀賞者進入另一純正美好的世界。他的彩墨繪畫藝術色彩豐滿沈穩，構圖新穎脫俗，敢爲人先，敢爲人無，融西方的無拘與東方的神秘于一體，藝術手法兼收並蓄，重新組合自己理想中的 "藝術王國" 模式，創出完全表現自我意識的新概念藝術理論，沖出傳統藝術手法和概念之藩籬，大膽采用以空靈世界爲主旨的藝術表現手法，閃射出智慧之光，泛溢出藝術才華，正如評論家所言 "關玉良的作品，所有顏色都是語言，所有墨調都有靈性，所有空間都充滿想象"。

關玉良說過："一個人一旦進入了藝術的大門，他就會不停地沿著藝術的規律去尋找、去建築、去發現、去觸摸、去創造，去表現他內心空間的情感，去追求生命的原點。"

關玉良的這一組 "中國娃" 畫作，正是畫家這些觀點的最佳體現，他用人類生命最爲原點的現象來诠釋人類的美好與歸宿。其實，藝術的本質正在於此。

國娃的誕生 Naissance of Guowa
世界唯／造型　The Only Shape in the word
中國唯／的陶瓷娃娃　The Only china Baby in China

# The Chinese Baby Full of WIT and Humor

Written by: Dong Yan
Translated by: Professor Pan Zongqian

Note: Chinese Baby (CB) is the name the artist gives to a series of paintings of child, he created. It is especially created in celebration of the coming Olympic Games.

Mr. Guan Yuliang, the famous painter of China, is praised by some as Picasso of the East. Any of his works invariably conceives abundant implication and a surprising vigor of art, which renders the viewer a great visual shaking.

In 2005, the series of painting under the name of "Chinese Baby" created by Guan Yuliang further show the artist's rich imagination and a superability of artistic expression, which is beyond description, and never to be forgotten. Though of identical theme, and of a relatively small size, the picture is by no means monotonous or dull, making those good at art appreciation utter exclamation about its marvelous taste—every of the pictures offers aftertaste, and at the same time, brings people into a reverie—in the bamboo basket are the wild fruits to be readily picked by people in the country; the upsticking queue of a charming naëve country girl, tied with the string twisted by her kind mother in the morning. The young girl, with sweet in her mouth, is tasting the freshness and sweet of life: in the hot summer, bamboo mat is the most ideal thing for them to have a fast sleep on, accompanied by a dreamy cat; the young girl's chubby body, slackened and sluggish, looks evidently a carefree young lass. She seems living a carefree life, primitive and idyllic, which is just the dreamy "fairy land" dreamt of by numberless people. Besides, in the great nature, there is free tripping and light dance, which goes along with the birds flying over. It is a joyful melody people can't help singing; the girl baby opens wide her watery eyes glistening pure and lovely like pearls. Besides her are the white doves of peace, impressing people with the similar purity and splendeur, in aspiration for peace and harmony in the human community. The girl baby, half opening her little mouth, seems to be uttering her call for peace.

Just as his works on other themes, this group of paintings of children of unique modeling by Guan Yuliang ushers the viewers into another pure and beautiful world. His inkcolor painting is rich in color, novel in modelling, dare to pioneer in what is never seen before, integrating the unstraintedness in the west painting with the mystory in the East. By way of incorporating the techniques of different styles and schools, Guan Yuliang makes up anew the pattern of his ideal "Kingdom of Art" As a result, he brings forth the art theory of a new conception which gives full expression of his self-awareness. This new theory breaks through the limit of the traditional artistic technique and conception, boldly adopts the highly abstract way of expression. It glistens with wisdom and brilliancy. Just as the commentator put it: "In Guan Yuliang's works each color represents a language, every tone of ink shows intelligence, all the spaces are full of imagination. "

Guan Yuliang said: "Once a person enters the world of art, he will set to search, to construct, to discover, to touch, to create, to give expression of his inner emotion, to find the origin of life."

The group painting of Chinese Baby is just the best manifestation of the artist's viewpoints. He gives interpretation to the wonder and ultimate future of mankind with the phenomena concerning the ultimate origin of life. In fact, that is just where the essence of art lies.

藝術家關玉良之子
－大山於法國

【國娃】陶瓷之三十
60CMX48CM
2006年

藝術家關玉良的夫人

# 收　藏　證

## 國娃出生證明

星座:北鬥星　　懷孕周期:2005~

出生年月日:2008年8月8日8時8分8秒　　身體狀況:優 + 優

出生地:中國·神秘的地方　　落戶地:中國·北京

族群戶主:關東·玉良　　學名:國娃

乳名:奧娃、神娃、武娃……　　身份證號:200808080808082008x

進京目的:登上奧運舞臺練一練、耍一耍　　申報項目:五項全能

心得體會:我參與、我奉獻、我快樂

## 國娃全球測試

測試日期:2007.08.08.08.08.08　　測試人數:2008人

生命指數:旺盛　　健康指數:正常（全身測試）

活力指數:無拘無束　　性格指數:野性、憨厚、善良

心理指數:陽光、開朗、極具愛心　　理想指數:健康、快樂

人氣指數：人見人愛　　官員指數:好看

專家指數:人格魅力、個性化　　商人指數:商機無限

文人指數：傳情、傳神　　藝術指數:東西文化的最佳結合點

美學指數:當代藝術、民族藝術　　收藏指數:世界唯一的陶娃娃

身價指數:陶瓷史的亮點　　幸運指數:奧運藝術史上唯一陶瓷娃娃

目標指數:跑遍全世界

題目:

_____

作者:

_____

創作年代:

_____

發證日期:

_____

# Birth Certificate of CB

Constellation: The BIG Dipper
Pregnancy period: 2005-Two thousand five
Time of birth: Year 2008, month 8, day 8, o'clock 8, minute 8
Health: good plus good
Birthplace: somewhere mysterious in China
The place to reside in: Beijing China
Head of the race: Yuliang from The Northeast
Formal name: Chinese Baby
Infant name: Ao-(Shen-Wu-)Wa
IC Number: 200808080808082008X
Why coming to Beijing: Mounting the Olympic stage to have a show
The event to take part in: Pentathlon
Understanding and experience: I particparte in, I make contribution, I feel happy.

# A Global Test of CB

Date of Testing: 2007.08.08.08.08.08
Number of the tested: 2008 People
Index of life: Thriving
Index of health: Normal, (an allover check)
Index of vigor: unconstrained
Index of character: Untamed, Simple, Kind
Index of psychology: Sunshine, Optimistic, kind
Index of ideal: Healthy and Happy
Index of popularity: Everyone loves it who sees it
In the eyes of officials: Nice-looking
In the eyes of specialists: Charming personality, Highly individualized
In the eyes of a merchant: boundless business opportunities
In the eyes of scholars: Vivid 、Lifelike
Index of art: The best point of conjuncture between the east and west culture
Index of aesthetics: Modern art, National art
Index of collection: The one and the only pottery baby in the world
Index of value: A glistening point in the history of pottery works exhibition
Index of fortune: The one and the only pottery figurine baby in Olympic art history

Title:
_____

Artist's
_____

Creation
Period: _____

Date of Lssue:
_____

# 關玉良生命的河

誰是關玉良？每個人有自己的定義。深圳大學藝術學院教授、國家一級畫家，國內外享有盛譽的藝術家，這是通俗的定義。他的藝術創作領域廣泛，自成一格，其雕塑、陶藝、重彩、水墨等藝術作品在海內外產生巨大影響；曾獲建國五十年文學藝術一等獎、法國蒙特羅市藝術獎章等十多項國內外藝術成就大獎；先後在國內外舉辦過30余次藝術展；出版個人藝術專著和作品集20多部，這是藝術圈的定義。他是一位極具愛心的人，近幾年來，他先後向國內外慈善組織捐贈數件藝術作品，爲兒童、助殘等公益事業籌集善款超千萬，這是愛心的定義。他是一位世界"新藝術"的探索者和苦行僧；他是一位行蹤神秘、性格古怪的藝術狂人；他是一位有強烈社會責任感的中國人，這是有關內心的定義。

關玉良自幼酷愛藝術，好讀傳記、哲學類書籍，喜歡聽薩克斯、提琴、長笛類演奏的悲壯名曲；做事專一，善解人意；抽有勁的香煙，習慣午夜用餐；喜歡騎馬，愛犬厭貓；最動情的是聽父母講過去的故事。

關玉良，國家一級美術師，滿族，黑龍江人，1957年生，畢業於哈爾濱師範大學藝術系，結業於中央美術學院國畫系，深圳大學藝術學院教授，北京中國畫研究院特聘畫家。在國際上成功舉辦個人畫展30余次，團體展50次之多。多次獲國內外大獎，走遍30多個國家，講學、交流，爲傳播民族文化盡心竭力。

他是九十年代突起的一位"重量級"藝術家，他以"無常規"的藝術創作理念思維達到了藝術作品的高峰期。

一九八八年，作爲首位東北藝術家進入中國台北三原色藝術中心。

一九九○年，作爲首個東北藝術家個人畫展進入韓國百想美術館，畫展獲得巨大成功，並獲"韓國國際藝術委員會特別畫家獎"。

同年，與香港畫廊簽約，他成爲了少數幸運者之一。

一九九二年，首個東北藝術家個人畫展進入美國紐約國際藝術中心，並獲"東方藝術創新獎"。

一九九三年，首個個人畫展在中國香港、北京、廣州、美國、哈爾濱展出。

一九九四年，作爲首個東北藝術家同英國畫廊簽約。

一九九五年，關玉良的個人畫展又進入一個高峰期，同年在英國、法國、加拿大、日本、韓國展出，並在中國香港拍賣公司拍出百萬元港幣的高價位。

至此，先後成爲《藝術界》、《中華博覽》、《華人風采》、《世界知識畫報》、《大家風采》、《現代美術》、《中國書畫博覽》等雜志的封面人物。

一九九○年，獲韓國現代美術大展"特別招待作家獎"。

一九九一年，獲韓國藝委會"中國現代優秀畫家獎"。

一九九二年，獲紐約國際藝術基金中心"東方藝術創新大獎"。

一九九四年，獲中國藝術博覽會三項大獎。

一九九七年，獲新加坡東方藝術成就大獎。

一九九九年，獲中華人民共和國文學藝術一等獎。

二○○一年，獲法國蒙特羅藝術獎。

二○○二年，獲深圳市十大品位男士。

二○○三年，作品《中國戲》是世界選美大賽慈善拍賣中，唯一一幅中國畫作品，並以高價位拍出。

二○○四年，又是他藝術創作巨大展示活動的高峰期。同年獲首屆中國收藏界年度排行榜十佳獎，又以特大貨櫃箱裝載600多件藝術品，在上海美術館、廣東美術館、中國美術館全面展示了"十年"來的藝術成就，並出版八本專著。

二○○六年，他是藝術界的幸運者，成爲得到第29屆北京奧運會組委會唯一授權，在國內外進行巡展的藝術家，將在國內十個城市中開展巡展活動。

二○○七年，獲中國殘疾人聯合會"文化助殘愛心大使"。

二○○七年，北京關玉良藝術工作室獲"第五屆北京2008"奧林匹克文化節中榮獲"參與獎"。

- 《關玉良繪畫藝術》　　　　　　　中國台灣三原色
- 《關玉良畫集》　　　　　　　　　韓國百想美術館
- 《關玉良畫集》　　　　　　　　　中國香港雲峰畫苑
- 《關玉良墨彩藝術》　　　　　　　黑龍江美術出版社
- 《關玉良藝術風‧墨彩集》　　　　黑龍江美術出版社
- 《關玉良藝術風‧墨象集》　　　　黑龍江美術出版社
- 《中國當代名家畫集‧關玉良》　人民美術出版社
- 《二十一世紀中國當代著名藝術家‧關玉良藝術風》
- 《論彩墨‧論水墨》　　　　　　　黑龍江美術出版社
- 《論人體‧論素描》　　　　　　　黑龍江美術出版社
- 《論文字‧論彩扇》　　　　　　　黑龍江美術出版社
- 《論陶藝‧論狀態》　　　　　　　黑龍江美術出版社
- 《當代備‧都市人》　　　　　　　黑龍江美術出版社
- 《人體藝術》　　　　　　　　　　黑龍江美術出版社
- 《關玉良奧運藝術作品集‧圓夢‧2008》
　　　　　　　　　　　　　　　　人民美術出版社
- 《圓夢‧2008國娃的誕生》　　　黑龍江美術出版社
- 《中國書畫博覽‧圓夢‧2008》　奧運專號‧中國書畫博覽雜志社

# Guan Yuliang's life — a River Surging Ever Forward

Who is Guan Yuliang? As to this question, each one has his own reply. Guan is a professor in the Art College under Shenzhen University, a first grade artist renowned both at home and abroad —— this is a general description of him.

But in the artistic circle, he is otherwise modified:he is an artist with a wide range of creation and a style of his own, involving sculpture, pottery art, heavy color, inkwash, etc. Over the years, he has won more than 10 art prizes at home and abroad, including the First Prize of Art on the occasion of the 50th anniversary of our Republic and a Prize of Art in Mentelo, France; he has held more than 30 art exhibitions at home and abroad, and has published more than 30 painting collections and monographs on art.

The charitable circle, on its part, may say something different about him. Guan is one with a loving heart. In recent years he has donated many of his artistic works to charitable organizations at home and abroad and has raised a large sum of money, more than ten million[RMB], for public good, say, to relieve the children and the disabled in dire conditions.

With regard to Guan's inner state, people say he is an ascetic devoted to the exploration of the world's "new art"; He is said to be an artmania, mysterious and eccentric; He is a Chinese with a strong sense of social responsibility.

From Guan's early childhood, he showed a keen interest in art. He liked reading, including reading biography and philosophy when he grew older. He enjoyed listening to famous melody performed with saxophone or flute. He always pays concentrated attention in doing a job; He is good at reading what others think and feel and is considerate. He usually smokes strong cigarettes, takes midnight meal, likes riding, likes dog but dislikes cat. What most touched him is listening to his parents telling him stories of the bygone days.

Guan Yuliang, a first-grade artist of the state, a Manchurian, was born in 1957. in Heilongjiang Province. He is a graduate of the art department under Heilongjiang Normal University. He has also studied in the Chinese painting department under China's Central Art Institute. He is now an art professor in Shenzhen University, a specially engaged painter by Beijing's Chinese Painting Research Institute. He has won major prizes again and again, and has travelled in more than 30 countries, giving lectures, communication and sparing no effort in spreading our national culture.

He is a prominent artist coming to the fore in the nineteen nineties. His artistic creation came to an upsurge under the guidance of his "abnormal" idea and thinking in creation.

In 1988. Guan, as the first artist from the Northeast, entered the Three Yuan Se Art Centre, in Taibei, China.

In 1990, Guan, as the first Northeast artist, entered Baixiang Gallery in South Korea, and won there a special painter prize from the Country's international Art Commission.

In the same year, Guan signed a contract with HongKong's Gallery, one among the lucky few.

In 1992, Guan, as the first Northeast artist, held his individual art exhibition at the international Art Centre in New York, U.S.A.

In the same year of 1993 Guan gave his first individual art exhibition successively in Hong Kong, Beijing, Guangzhou, America, Harbin.

In 1994, Guan, as the first Northeast artist, signed a contract with the British Gallery.

In 1995, Guan was busy in holding his individual painting exhibitions in Britain, France, Canada, Japan, South Korea, and his art works were auctioned at a high price of one million HK dollars at the auctioneer's company.

Guan's photos have been published on the covers of more than eight magazines,such as 《Artistic Circle》, 《Modern Art》 etc.

The following is a list of the prizes he won over the years:

1990, Guan was awarded a special prize at South Korea's Grand Modern Art Exhibition.

1991, Guan was awarded the prize of China's Excellent Modern Painter by South Korea's Art committee.

1992, Guan was awarded the "Oriental Art Trail-Blazing Prize" by New York's International Art Center.

1994, Guan was awarded the three major prizes at China's Art Fair.

1997, Guan was awarded the Oriental Art Achievement Prize at Singapore.

1999, Guan was awarded the Art and literature First Prize of PRC.

2001, Guan was awarded the Art Prize at Mentalo, France.

2002, Guan's painting 《The Chinese Drama》 is the only Chinese painting found in the charitable auction together with the World Beauty Selection and was auctioned at a high price.

2004, this year witnessed another height in Guan's artistic creation. In this year, Guan received a 10-merit prize that China's collection circle awarded for the first time. Besides, more than 100 pieces of his art creation loaded in a superlarge contaniner were transported and displayed at the galleries in Shanghai, Guangdong and Beijing. They presented an all-sided picture of his artistic achievements over the past 10 years.

2006, he is a lucky fellow in the art circle as he is the sole one authorized by the Olympic Organizational Committee to hold his touring art exhibition at home or abroad in the name of Olympic. It will be arranged in ten cities in China.

2007, he is awarded the title of "the Ambassador with a loving heart in helping the disabled", conferred by China Disabled Persons Federation.

The following are Guan Yuliang's publications of art over these years.

《Guan Yuliang's art of Painting》 by SanYuanSi, Taiwan, China

《A Collection of Paintings of Guan Yuliang》 by Bai Xian Gallery, South Korea

《A Collection of Paintings of Guan Yuliang》 by Hong Kong Yan Fan Painting Centre.

《Guan Yuliang's Inkcolor Art》 by Art Publishing House, Heilongjiang

《Guan Yuliang's Artistic Style·Inkclor Collection》 Art Publishing House, Heilongjing

《Guan Yuliang's Artistic Style·Inkclor Collection》 Art Publishing House, Heilongjing

《Painting Collection of the Famous Painter Guan Yuliang》 People's Art Publishing House

《Famous Artist of the 21st century·Guan Yuliang's Art Style》

《On Inkcolor and Inkwash》 Art Publishing House, Heilongjiang

《On Human body·on sketch》 Art Publishing House, Heilongjiang

《On Words·On Color Painted Fan》 Art Publishing House, Heilongjiang

《On Pottery·On State》 Art Publishing House, Heilongjiang

《The Modern Servant,The Urban People》 Art Publishing House, Heilongjiang

《Art of Human Body》 Art Publishing House,Heilongjiang

《China's Modern Famous Artist,Dream Coming True 2008》 People's Art Publishing House

《Dream Coming True. 2008, How the Baby Chinese comes to Birth》 Art Publishing House, Heilongjiang

《Display of China's Books and Paintings, Dreaming Coming True, 2008》 The special issue of the magazine 《The Display of China's Books and Paintings》

藝術家關玉良先生與夫人

**圖書在版編目（CIP）數據**

圓夢2008關玉良：國娃的誕生／關玉良著.—哈爾濱：
黑龍江美術出版社,2007.08
（二十一世紀中國當代著名藝術家關玉良藝術風）
ISBN 978-7-5318-1921-9

Ⅰ.圓… Ⅱ.關… Ⅲ.藝術—作品綜合集—中國—現代
Ⅳ.J121

中國版本圖書館CIP數據核字（2007）第123062號

二十一世紀中國當代著名藝術家關玉良藝術風
# 圓夢2008關玉良·國娃的誕生

| | |
|---|---|
| 著 | 關玉良 |
| 責任編輯 | 徐曉麗 李正剛 |
| 出　版 | 黑龍江美術出版社 |
| 社　址 | 哈爾濱市道裏區安定街225號 |
| 郵政編碼 | 150016 |
| 電　話 | 0451-84270525 84270511 |
| 經　銷 | 全國新華書店 |
| 網　址 | www.hljmss.com.cn |
| 印　刷 | 深圳市國際彩印有限公司 |
| 開　本 | 787×1092 1/16 |
| 印　張 | 6 |
| 版　次 | 2007年8月第1版 |
| 印　次 | 2007年8月第1次印刷 |
| 書　號 | ISBN 978-7-5318-1921-9 |
| 定　價 | 98.00元 |